Scrapbooks of America™

Published by Tradition Books™ and distributed to the school and library market by The Child's World®
P.O. Box 326, Chanhassen, MN 55317-0326 ➝ 800/599-READ ➝ http://www.childsworld.com

An Editorial Directions book
Editors: E. Russell Primm and Lucia Raatma
Additional Writing: Lucia Raatma and Alice Flanagan/Flanagan Publishing Services
Photo Selector: Lucia Raatma
Photo Researcher: Alice Flanagan/Flanagan Publishing Services
Proofreader: Chad Rubel
Design: Kathleen Petelinsek/The Design Lab

Library of Congress Cataloging-in-Publication Data
Dell, Pamela.
The gold coin : a story about New York City's Lower East Side / by Pamela J. Dell.
p. cm. — (Scrapbooks of America series)
Includes index.
Summary: In 1901, thirteen-year-old Dimitri, his younger brother, and their parents are beginning to feel at home in New York City's Lower East Side, where they have lived since their Jewish faith led them to flee Russia thirteen months earlier.
ISBN 1-59187-017-8 (library bound : alk. paper)
[1. Immigrants—Fiction. 2. Jews—New York (N.Y.)—Fiction. 3. Russian Americans—Fiction. 4. Coins—Collectors and collecting—Fiction. 5. New York (N.Y.)—History—1898–1951—Fiction.] I. Title.
PZ7.D3845 Go 2002
[Fic]—dc21   2002004769

Scrapbooks of America™

THE GOLD COIN

A Story of New York's Lower East Side and Its Immigrants

by Pamela Dell

TRADITION BOOKS™
EXCELSIOR, MINNESOTA

TABLE OF CONTENTS

Dimitri's Story, page 6

"One year and already you are so much an American boy I cannot recognize you, Dimitri! Not even in my **spectacles!**" my father said to me. He did not sound happy. He turned to look upon my brother next. "And my son Rueven—even worse!"

Mama, Papa, Rueven, and I were leaving Walhalla Hall, a place that was like the beating heart of our new life in a new world. Walhalla was the meeting place for our family and others like us, Jews who had left the Russian homeland to find something better in America. To that hall, which stood on the corner of Hester and Orchard Streets on New York's Lower East Side, we would come to talk and sing and to make new friends. There, children studied their lessons while their parents argued over articles in the news and traded gossip. They planned ways to improve working conditions in the **sweatshops** and other factories. Often Walhalla was the place we gathered to remember together our old life, too. But to me, that old life already seemed distant and hard to recall, as if it had happened to some other boy.

I was a different boy now, a boy who had lived for thirteen months in a crowded neighborhood known as the tenth ward. It was a neighborhood of more than 75,000 people, so many people! People from all over the world crammed together in a few long city blocks and all hoping to find their dream of freedom and safety. Whenever Papa began his moans of how American my brother and

The Lower East Side
is defined by these
boundaries: Fourteenth
Street to the north,
Catherine Street to
the south, Broadway
to the west, and the
East River to the east.

The Lower East Side was a crowded, noisy, exciting place for us to live.

I were becoming, these were the thoughts that rose in my head.

"Rueven even worse!" Papa repeated, bringing me back to the present. Rueven caught my eye, and we tried not to laugh. But my father was right. Rueven had eased into his American life even more effortlessly and more quickly than I. He seemed to have come from a different part of our ancestry than the rest of us. Papa, Mama, and I were all small-boned and dark. Rueven was much sturdier in build, with hair the color of a wild pumpkin. At only twelve—twelve! A year younger than I—he was already half an inch taller and, according to Papa, built like our grandfather Lev Domashevsky.

Already Rueven knew well the ins and

Walhalla Hall was a place where dances and weddings were held, and adults had important meetings there, too.

Like this bread maker, people sold all sorts of items on Orchard Street.

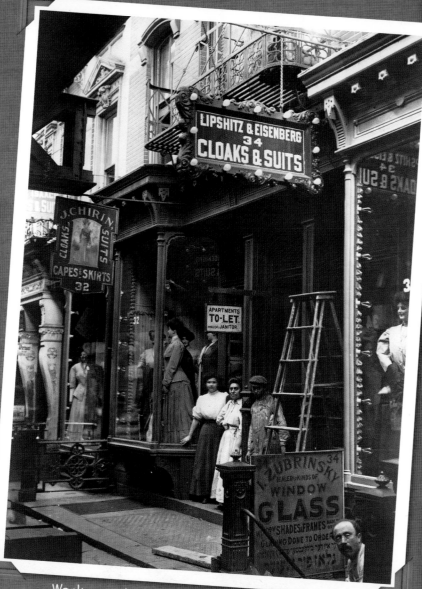

Workers outside one of the many sweatshops that operated in our neighborhood

outs of those tangled Lower East Side streets. He had even made friends with boys who were not Jewish, a shock to Mama. I could not tell her or Papa that the minute we were away from them, Rueven would pull the **yarmulke,** his skullcap, from his head and stuff it into his pocket. This would have shocked both of them even more and worried them into sleeplessness at night, too.

I did not think it so bad that maybe Rueven was a little different from the rest of us. Was it good that we should all be the same? Like the dozens of shirts that came from the sewing machines, one after another, at the sweatshops? All the same, all the same. I was not in favor of that. I wanted to see a factory where all the shirts came out differently, each one a surprise, with new secrets to discover. Just as I felt it should be with people. All that was important to me was that Rueven and I were cut from the same cloth.

✡

Mama and Papa walked ahead of us as we moved down Hester Street and cut over to Grand. I had spent the hours at Walhalla that morning studying hard my mathematics lesson. Now it was good to be outside again. I didn't mind that it was nearly as hot on the streets as in the stuffy, baking heat of the brick buildings. I liked the blinding brightness of the early afternoon light after the dimness of being inside. We were having an early fall heat

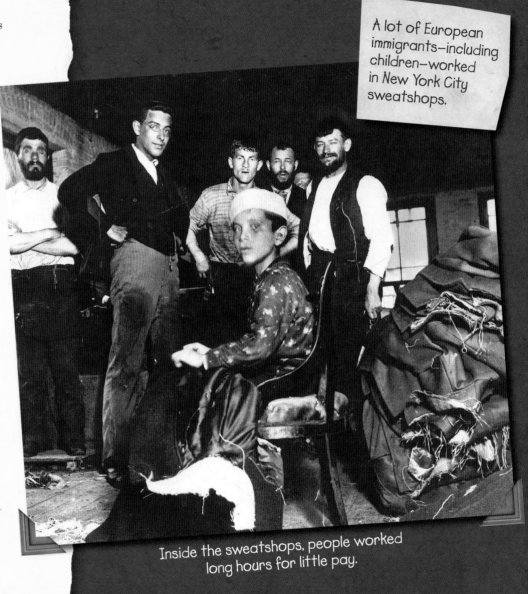

A lot of European immigrants—including children—worked in New York City sweatshops.

Inside the sweatshops, people worked long hours for little pay.

wave, the newspapers said, and to me it was all good.

The corner of Rivington and Orchard Streets, where pushcarts offered so many different items for sale

There on those streets, an area known as the Pig Market, it was as if twenty circuses were taking place at once. It was a place teeming with horse-drawn wagons, pushcarts, and **peddlers.** There were garment shops, bakeries, and butchers. There was cloth for sale and ribbons of every color. Pushcarts full of carrots and potatoes and turnips, apples and figs and strange yellow things called bananas. Strangely enough, the only thing that could not be bought in the Pig Market was a pig itself,

Each Friday evening, we lit candles and ate challah
bread to celebrate our Sabbath.

because eating pork was against Jewish law.

As we walked that day, the **cobble-stone** streets of the Pig Market were filled with people. So many people that it was impossible to move forward without being bumped on every side. It was difficult even to hear one's own voice for the shouts of the **vendors,** all rising together in a hundred different languages. Babies screamed against the heat. The smells of fresh bread, fish, leather, and pickles all mingled together in the autumn air. For me, to be in the middle of so much *mishegas,* so much craziness, was a good time always.

Good also was that it was Friday today.

The tenth ward contained 1,179 tenement houses in 1900 and was home to 15,132 families. That year, its total population was 76,073 people! Some said it was the most densely populated place on Earth.

That meant *shabbat,* the **Sabbath,** would begin at sunset. Once the sun went down and the shabbat candles were burning, no shopping or working was allowed. Not even did we light our own lamps then. But beside the fine meal we would enjoy, I loved shabbat for another reason. Each week on that night, the Russian boy I had been came close to me again and kept me from forgetting him entirely.

As we made our way along the streets, Mama picked out the ingredients for the shabbat meal. She chose bread—a plump **challah**—and bargained with a peddler for a nice piece of fish. Papa waved to a friend and wished him Happy New Year. According

to the Jewish calendar, we were approaching
the year 5662, even though the American
calendar told us the date was mid-September
1901.

Walking beside Rueven, I felt a sudden
shot of energy fly through my arms and legs.
I had had enough of sitting and being quiet.
I wanted to run and shout. I wanted to send
chords of wild music into the air with my
violin.

I took off and instantly Rueven was at
my heels. Mama called to us to be careful, to
stay with them, but we paid little attention.
Our parents continued through the **throng,**
but Rueven and I wove in and out among
the dozens of pushcarts crowding the curbs,
playing a game of tag. Part of our game was

A Jewish New Year card, for a
holiday we celebrated each autumn

On holidays, we often played with a dreidel, a four-sided toy that spins like a top. On each of the four sides is a Hebrew letter: Nun, Gimel, Hay, and Shin. The letters stand for the phrase Nes Gadol Hayah Sham, which means "a great miracle happened there."

Poor living conditions in Russia and unfair treatment by the government forced many of us to leave our country and travel to America.

to stay near our parents but not too close.

Finally, though, two blocks from home, Papa demanded we walk beside them and behave as "respectable" human beings. As we ran to join them, Rueven and I spoke to each other in rapid English sentences. It was a language our parents were still far from mastering. Whenever we spoke in this way, Papa would grouse at us in **Yiddish,** saying we made him feel old and tired and dumb as an ox.

But really, he was still young and strong and smart. Strong and smart enough, anyway, to have found us all a way safely out of Russia before we were separated and imprisoned, or worse. If Papa had been drafted into the Russian

15

army, he would have had to serve the **czar**

for twenty-five years. Until I was thirty-eight

years old! We might have been sent to a work

camp for studying books or for teaching

someone to write or for trying to buy a plot

of our own land. But we were in America

now, where we could do all these things

without being sent to prison or death.

"I should be so lucky to have boys who

are thinking of God instead of games!" Papa

said as we came up obediently behind them

at last, out of breath and finally quiet. He

shook his head as if he were the saddest man

on earth and his long **earlocks** brushed his

cheeks. Rueven grinned widely, obviously

enjoying Papa's *kvetching*, his complaining.

"Not to get upset, Zev," Mama said softly,

16

Just like this man, we entered the United States through the immigration center at Ellis Island.

Jewish people follow the basic laws and teachings of Judaism, which come from the Torah, the first five books of the Hebrew Bible.

The Lower East Side had row after row of tenement houses.

laying a hand on Papa's arm. Whenever Mama spoke to Papa in this way, I knew she was remembering the terrors we had left. She would be thinking thoughts of gratitude, even though we were living one on top of another and no fresh stream flowed just beyond our windows. She was thinking, as she always did, of the bright side. We had escaped the **pogroms,** the killings of the Jews, in our hometown of Tula in the Russian Pale. We were gone from there, and safe.

We turned down Norfolk Street, our street. In the middle of the block was a six-story brick **tenement** that had a **kosher** meat market on the first floor. Above it, on the fourth floor, was our apartment. It was a little home of three rooms, with a single window that looked down on the street. That window brought in noise at all hours of the day and night. But we thought ourselves a fortunate family to live in a building with lights and a toilet. We had to share our bathroom with four other families, it was true, but many of the other tenements had only an **outhouse** in back and no electric lights at all.

It was good to have those small comforts, yes, but as we arrived home, the last thing I wanted to do was go inside again. I did not want to spend the afternoon in those dark and **sweltering** rooms.

"I am going to practice!" I called, bounding up the narrow, rickety stairs ahead of them all. I hurried to the tiny room—more

Some people called the tenth ward "New Israel" because so many Russian and Eastern European Jews had moved there.

like a closet—that Rueven and I shared. It was in the back of the apartment, next to the even tinier kitchen. It had no window but only an opening to an airshaft at the center of the building. I grabbed my violin case from the corner, then stopped for a moment to sit on the cot where I slept. Lifting a loose floorboard beneath the cot, I brought out a cotton handkerchief, its corners tied together. I untied it and emptied its contents onto my bed. In the dim light of a lit candle, I began to count: seven dollars and twenty-three cents in change. It was a fortune! Plus three strange old coins, the precious beginning of my coin collection. Even as I held them in my palm, feeling their

Inside the tenements, the apartments were often small and dark.

weight, it was hard to believe those three coins were really mine. Yet how I had come to have them was even more surprising. It was a tale I hadn't yet told to anyone.

I tucked my treasure away again and headed out of the apartment just as Mama and Papa were coming in. From below in the stairwell, Rueven shouted to me impatiently in English.

"Come on, Dimitri! Let's go!"

He had gotten into the habit of often coming with me when I went off to find a spot in the cool breezes to play my violin. When there was time, we went to Corlears Hook, a real park that even

New York City parks were full of activity.

The East River Bridge was built over the East River to connect Manhattan with Brooklyn.

had bits of grass between the benches. From there, we could gaze out at the East River and watch the **billowing** sails of the boats as they passed by. There we could see the huge East River Bridge and watch the wealthy men strolling in their top hats. It was a peaceful place, and well worth visiting, though it was many blocks from home. When we were lucky, Rueven and I would catch a ride there with the wagon drivers who carted blocks of ice back and forth for the Knicker-bocker Ice Company.

At Corlears Hook, Rueven rode the scooter he had made for himself from the wood of an orange crate and the discarded wheels of an old pair of roller skates. He had

21

polished the wood with oil. Then he had nailed a scrap of brass that Papa had given him to the wood. In this way alone, Rueven took after Papa. He had hammered his name in Hebrew into the brass plate and added the image of a pine cone hanging from the bough, to remind him of the pines in Russia, he said. He had done all this with an artist's skill that nearly matched our father's.

Papa had been the most respected **samovar** craftsman in all of Tula. There he worked in the best of the metalworking factories, making fine brass and silver samovars and the delicate teapots that rest upon them. Now he shared

When we left Russia, Czar Nicholas II was in power.

These boys are ready to race their scooters, homemade ones just like Rueven's.

Papa made beautiful items like this brass samovar.

a shop with another Tula immigrant in Allen Street. That street was known as Brass Town, for more than 300 metalworking shops crowded that street, one after another along its entire length. But even among so many others, Papa was a master craftsman.

"Like father, like son!" Papa had proclaimed proudly on seeing Rueven's handi-work. "But to City College you will be going! You will be educated. Your father, he works for nothing else, remember that!"

This outburst had made Rueven laugh—Rueven, whose scooter was his most prized possession. Being able to get from one block to another on wheels was the thing he cared about more than nearly everything else. At our spot by the river, he would ride that scooter up and down, up and down the walking path, while I played. That spot was where my own most prized possession, the three coins, had come to me from the odd old man.

✡

Now, as we clambered together down the dark stairs to the street, Mama's voice floated down to our ears.

"Dimitri! Rueven! Watch out for the *vildachaya!*" she warned, speaking Yiddish in a sharp voice. The **hooligans,** she would have said, if she had known the English word. She meant the rough boys who lived in the neighborhood, too. The boys in the tenth ward were mostly Jewish boys, from places like Russia and Poland. But in the surrounding wards

Before Ellis Island opened in 1892, immigrants to America were processed at Castle Garden in lower Manhattan.

lived boys who came from Ireland and Italy and many other places besides. And all of them frightened Mama for being so unfamiliar to her.

"Nothing but *vildachaya* there are here, from all over the world!" Mama moaned each time we left the building to play. "On these very streets!"

But I was not planning to live on these streets forever. I would be rich someday and own a big house, with tall pine trees in the back garden. My old coins would grow into a fat heap and make the dream come true. The old man had told me so.

✡

The air at Corlears Hook was as refreshing as

slipping into the water at the public baths. I settled on a bench and stared out at the dark river streams for a moment before pulling out my violin. The sun glinted in diamond sparkles on the water's surface, making me want to play a bright, happy tune. I put the violin to my chin and began.

The first day it had happened by accident. Ever since then, it had all been on purpose. I had just discovered Corlears Hook and had come that day alone to practice. It was a bright day at the end of spring. I took up my violin, leaving its case open on the bench beside me. I began to play a piece that reminded me of the slow and magical movement of the river. It was deep and **somber** with a few unexpected hurried spots, like the river itself.

Many people were strolling along in the warm sunshine that afternoon. Suddenly a handsomely dressed man came toward the bench and dropped a few pennies into my violin case. I was so shocked I stopped playing at once. I tried to protest and return the money

With my violin, I made music that I began to share with the people of Corlears Hook.

25

to him. I was not begging, I told him. He insisted I keep the pennies and those standing near nodded in agreement.

"Think of yourself as a performer," he had told me, "an artist who deserves it. Above all, keep playing." Many others spoke up then, too, saying that my music made their afternoon stroll even better. Someone else dropped in a nickel. And then another coin came and another. I played for an hour and could not believe the heaviness of the change that filled my pockets as I walked home.

After that, whenever I was able, I came to play at the river. Over the summer months, I began to build my fortune. Then one late afternoon, an old man sat down at the far end of my bench. I was playing the saddest sounding song I knew, for I was sad. I had been awake all night, wondering if Papa would be forever struggling to pay our bills. And if we should ever again really be so lucky to live under trees and perhaps near a stream. It seemed that we never would.

When I had finished my tune that day, the old man nodded his white head and said in Yiddish, "*Zair gut!* Excellent!" Then he tossed a coin into my case, got up, and walked away.

For three days this occurred, the same old man sitting at the other end of the bench and leaving me a coin each time. But these coins were different from all the others I had been earning. Each of these looked older than someone's great-great-grandfather and they

The coins Mr. Zinkoff gave me were special, and his shop was full of old and valuable pieces.

had writing on them that was neither Hebrew nor English. On the third day, when he again pitched his coin into the case, he looked at me intently for a moment and then spoke.

"These coins I have given you," he said. "They have some value."

I stopped and looked at him. "They do?" Before he had said this, I had believed them to be just interesting old pieces of copper.

The old man nodded slowly. "Take care not to lose them, and someday a rich man you will be for having them," he said. "Come to my shop and you will see many more. Beautiful, priceless coins, some of them." He wrote down an address on East Tenth Street and handed it to me. I stared at it a long time, and when I looked up, he was gone.

Between 1881 and 1914, more than two million Jews left Russia. Many of them came to America like us.

That had happened a month before, and my thoughts of the old man now were interrupted by Rueven's shouts.

"Dimitri!" he called to me. "Look!" He was coursing down the pathway, his sturdy-looking arms flung to each side. The scooter was balanced perfectly on its small wheels as it moved forward. Once he had told Papa he might like to be a boxer when he grew up. It was an idea put into his head by his friend Sandro, a boy who had

Rueven sometimes spoke of being a boxer, like these boys who trained at the local gymnasium.

recently arrived in the tenth ward from Italy. Papa and Mama both were so upset by this that they nearly fainted one on top of the other.

"Your mother you're trying to kill or what?!" Papa shouted. "And what about me, your father?! You want I should work twelve hours a day so my son can go into the ring with a human bull? A bull who will box away his brains? Never!" Rueven only laughed. There was little that ever upset his good-natured temperament.

I waved at him now as he sailed past. Farther up the path, I could see two older boys watching him, too. They glanced over at me, and I turned back to playing. In my mind, I saw the new coin I was going to buy with the money I was earning and saving.

A week after the old man had given me the address of his shop, I had gone there. It was a tiny place in the midst of the Yiddish theater district. The neighborhood was lively with young people, exciting. Cafés on every corner, and every café filled with actors and workers from the sweatshops and the vegetable markets. All talking at once. All shouting and laughing and drinking sweet lemon-scented Russian tea.

The old man's shop had a sign in the window that read:

Julius Zinkoff. Rare Coins. Cigars. Trinkets.

It seemed a strange mix of items for a single shop to sell, but I went in. It was a dusty place, filled with old glass display cases full of all kinds of strange things. Buttons and tin matchboxes. Small pocket knives. But especially coins. Heaps of coins. Mr. Zinkoff showed me coins from every corner of the world. So many I could not have decided which I would buy first if I had been able to afford even one. But just as I was about to leave, Mr. Zinkoff pointed out a coin in a locked case. It shone like a small golden sun and was nearly a hundred years old, he told me. One of the earliest American coins, he said. Made at the Philadelphia **mint,** when that mint had been the only one in the country. Now there were three mints, Mr. Zinkoff explained. "That coin in a collection could change a man's fortune one day," he hinted.

30

Mr. Zinkoff told me that the value of a coin depends on two factors—its condition and how easy or hard it is to get.

Mr. Zinkoff's shop was on a busy section of East Tenth Street.

All the way home that day, I thought about that little gold piece. I thought about how long it would take to earn the money to have it for my own. I knew that coin would go a long way to making me a rich man.

I thought about that coin again now as I sat on the bench at Corlears Hook. My bow slid effortlessly over the strings, sending up round, full notes into the air. I played one of the tunes I knew best. Its beautiful melody always brought me many pennies and nickels and even a dime or two. I had nearly all the money I needed by then, and if I was lucky that day, then on Monday that coin in Mr. Zinkoff's locked case would be mine.

When the Brooklyn Bridge opened in 1883, at least 1,800 vehicles crossed it on the first day.

As I was playing, the crowd began to thin away and I saw two older boys walking toward me. Their faces were dirty. They wore scuffed boots and clothes that badly needed washing. One even had whiskers.

"Hey you, you little pip-squeak!" the whiskered one said to me as they approached. From the way he pronounced his English, I was certain he was not from the tenth ward. I snapped shut my violin case before they could see how much change was lying there. I watched them cautiously as they came to stand right in front of me.

"What are you doin' down here all alone, banging away on that silly, stupid fiddle?" the other one said, his eyes narrowing. Both of their mouths were turned up in ugly smirks.

"It's a violin," I replied. They were looming over me now. I squirmed off the end of the bench and stood up, violin and bow in one hand, my case in the other. Still, they pressed in toward me.

"What's in your case, tune boy? Money?"

"No!" I said. But they were breathing in my face and I backed up two steps. Then one of them reached out and pushed

Most of the boys outside the tenth ward were hard workers, like these bread peddlers on Mulberry Street. But others, like those who chased us at the park that day, were just bullies.

me, so that I stumbled back another few steps.

"Give me that thing!" the whiskered one growled.

"No!" I shouted. I pulled my violin and the case in to my chest, but it was hard to hold everything and I dropped my bow. The taller boy, the one with the pointed chin and no whiskers, reached down and quickly grabbed the bow. He whacked my leg with it and laughed when I jumped.

I tried to see where Rueven was, but the two older boys were so big I couldn't see past them. The tall boy slapped me again with the bow, a sharp stinging this time against my arm. I felt a painful pulsing begin in my temple.

"Get away from me!" I shouted. My words were like a lash of their own. The minute I screamed this out, they both lunged for me, but I held on furiously to my violin and its case. Then suddenly, just as one of them was about to wrench the case from my grasp, he howled and whirled around.

Behind him, I could see Rueven now running toward us. He was pelting them with a whirlwind of small stones as he came. Farther away, his scooter was lying in a patch of grass. Before I could even blink, Rueven had jumped on the back of the closest boy. He hooked an arm around the boy's neck and began to punch him in the shoulder with his free hand. The boy twirled, losing his balance, and at last Rueven jumped off his back. Stunned, the boy fell to his knees, not even able to grab hold of my stocky little brother.

Rueven and I managed to get away from the boys by disappearing into the busy market.

"Run, Dimitri!" Rueven shouted. "Run for the Pig Market!" But I was frozen, watching him as his fist slammed into the stomach of the other boy, the whiskered one. The boy doubled over, too. The next second Rueven was running toward me. He stopped to scoop up the dropped bow, then grabbed the violin from me. I held tightly to the handle of my case, and together we flew away from Corlears Hook.

We ran for two blocks before I looked back over my shoulder. The older boys were still in sight, but way behind us. One of them was carrying Rueven's scooter under his arm.

"Rueven!" I shouted, with the last breath left in my lungs. "They have your scooter!" Rueven almost stopped as he looked back, too. There was a moment of hesitation, as if he were thinking of going back. Then he shook his head.

"Come on," he said. I could hear the disappointment in his voice. "I don't want to fight those guys."

We blasted up Division Street, cut over to Hester, our feet as if on fire from running so fast. Soon we were swallowed up by the chaos of the Pig Market, its sounds and sights as overpowering as ever. Ducking behind a grocer's barrel of **pungent** green pickles, we waited. Soon the two boys appeared, their heads bobbing

Violins were first played in the 1500s. They were developed from early bowed instruments that may have been used by Chinese musicians as early as A.D. 900.

among the crowd across the street. They scanned the faces, straining to find us. But we were not to be found. As we watched from our hiding place, the taller boy raised his fist, cursing the air. Then his companion shouted in an angry voice that they would be back one day soon. Then they turned and headed off.

It was nearly sunset, the Sabbath. Rueven and I stood from behind the barrel and ran for home.

✡

That night again it was too hot to sleep indoors. We hauled the bedding from the fire escape where Mama draped it each morning to air. We climbed to the roof to sleep under the stars, all of us together, and many other families in the building, too.

When we were sure Mama and Papa were deep asleep, Rueven and I began to go over the details of the day in whispers. We discussed again the part where Papa had become upset to learn that Rueven's scooter had been stolen. We had not mentioned that we had been way over at Corlears Hook. We both knew that Mama would have kept us in the house for a month had she known that.

"It's just gone," Rueven had told Papa at supper, holding out his hands, palms up. "What do you want I should do about it, cry?"

Now there in the darkness on the roof, he repeated the main point, softly. "It's gone." This time, though, his voice was missing the "who cares" tone it had held when he told Papa. Now his voice was truly full of longing

Almost 90 percent of the Jews in Europe spoke Yiddish during the late 1800s and early 1900s.

When the weather was too hot, our family and others often slept on the tenement roof.

for his fine set of wheels. He sighed deeply and turned over, away from me. In a minute, I heard the even breath of his sleep.

I lay there, the only one awake now, and stared up at the stars. I thought of my golden coin, locked away in Mr. Z's shop. I knew I had enough money now to buy it. The coin that would take me so far in becoming a wealthy man. It seemed a magic charm in my imagination.

But I had seen something else a few days earlier in the window of another shop, not far from Mr. Z's. Something that was also stirring my imagination now. Something rare and beautiful and whose price was nearly the same as the gold coin.

> The first bicycles had solid tires of rubber or iron. But by the time we saw bicycles, their tires were filled with air.

As I lay there looking at the stars, I made my decision. I would take my earnings and buy that thing in the other shop window instead. It was a thing so new that it would make me the first boy in the whole tenth ward to bring one home.

Someday I might still own that coin, I thought, and I might very well become a rich man. But for now, I would be rich in another way. I would go to that shop and buy that thing—a two-wheeled bicycle—and bring it home to Rueven. And when I gave it to him, I would feel rich in knowing we were brothers cut from the same cloth.

Lady Humber

HUMBER CYCLES

NOT CHEAP BUT GOOD

BEALL & FISHER, AGENTS
1402 14th STREET, N. W.

Buying a bicycle for Rueven would make me feel richer than owning any gold coin ever could.

THE HISTORY OF IMMIGRANTS IN NEW YORK'S LOWER EAST SIDE

In 1900, Dimitri Domashevsky's family arrived in the United States and settled on New York City's Lower East Side. They joined the mass of immigrants living in overcrowded apartment buildings called tenements. Between 1881 and 1914, more than a million Russian Jews emigrated to the United States. Years of discrimination and violent attacks against them in Russia had forced them to leave their homeland to find a better life.

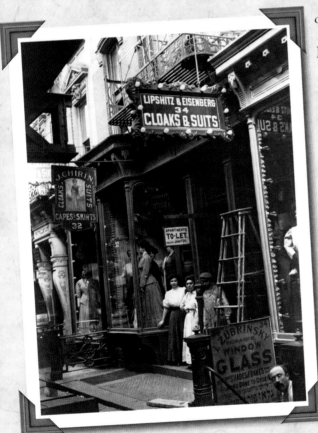

Unable to own land in Russia or work as farmers, most Jews could only make a living as shopkeepers or merchants. After coming to New York City, many Jews found work in the clothing industry as tailors and seamstresses. They worked long hours cramped into small, stuffy rooms called sweatshops. Others worked outside selling dry goods such as ribbons and rags. Some sold fruit and vegetables. They pushed heavily loaded carts through the busy streets while yelling out their wares. Eventually, some of the hard-working peddlers managed to save enough money to open small stores. By 1889, the Lower East Side was a hive of business activity. There were hundreds of grocery stores, butcher shops, and candy stores. There was even a daily newspaper and a theater.

Over time, Jewish immigrants distinguished themselves in the arts and sciences. They became entertainers, writers, artists, and patrons of the arts. Many musicians, such as Irving Berlin, who wrote "God Bless America," and George and Ira Gershwin, grew up on the Lower East Side. Today, more than one-third of all Jews in the United States live in New York City. It remains the principal port of entry and settlement site for new Jewish immigrants coming into the United States from all over the world.

GLOSSARY

billowing swelling and moving in the wind

challah bread that is usually braided or twisted before baking and traditionally eaten by Jews on the Sabbath and holidays

chords groups of three or more musical tones sounded at the same time

cobblestone a round stone once used in large numbers to make streets

czar the title of Russian rulers before the 1917 revolution

earlocks curls of hair hanging in front of a person's ears, common among Orthodox Jewish men

hooligans bullies or troublemakers

kosher prepared according to Jewish law

mint a place where metal is made into coins, usually under government authority

outhouse a bathroom that is not connected to the main building

peddlers people who carry goods from place to place and offer them for sale

pogroms organized killings of innocent people

pungent having a strong smell or taste

TIMELINE

1881 A wave of pogroms in Russia leads to a large number of Jewish citizens emigrating to the United States.

1883 The Brooklyn Bridge opens and links Brooklyn to Manhattan.

1886 The Statue of Liberty is erected in New York Harbor, a symbol welcoming immigrants to the United States.

1891 A law is passed that expels all Jews from Moscow, though they had been settled in that Russian city since 1865.

1892 Ellis Island opens as an immigration station in New York Harbor.

1894 Nicholas II, Russia's last czar, comes to power.

1898 New York becomes the second most populated city in the world, behind only London.

Sabbath a day of the week devoted to worship; Saturday is the Sabbath for Jews whereas Sunday is the Sabbath for most Christians.

samovar an urn with a spout at its base, used especially in Russia to boil water for tea

somber dark and gloomy

spectacles an old-fashioned term for eyeglasses

sweatshops factories in which workers are employed for long hours at low wages and under unhealthy conditions

sweltering very hot

tenement an apartment house, usually one that is overcrowded and usually having five or six stories

throng a big crowd

vendors people who sell goods to others

yarmulke a cap that fits over the base of one's skull, usually worn by Orthodox and Conservative Jewish males

Yiddish a German language written in Hebrew letters, spoken by Jewish people and their descendants of central and Eastern European origin

1901 Nearly 70 percent of New York's population lives in tenements. A tenement law is passed requiring these buildings to provide more light and air.

1904 The Jewish Museum opens, beginning with a collection of books and other objects from Judge Mayer Sulzberger. The museum is initially housed at the Jewish Theological Seminary library.

1911 On March 21, the worst factory fire in New York history breaks out at the Triangle Shirtwaist Company on Rivington Street in the Lower East Side. Because the factory doors are locked to keep the immigrant workers at their sewing machines, 146 die in less than twenty minutes. Most of the dead are young Russian women.

1947 The Jewish Museum moves to a new location on Fifth Avenue, the former mansion of businessman Felix Warburg.

ACTIVITIES

Continuing the Story

(Writing Creatively)

Continue Dimitri's story. Elaborate on an event from his scrapbook or add your own

entries to the beginning or end of his journal. You might write about Dimitri's life in Tula,

Russia, before his family emigrated to the United States, or how he developed his talent as

a violin player in the United States. You can also write your own short story of historical

fiction about Jewish immigrants living on New York's Lower East Side in the early 1900s.

Celebrating Your Heritage

(Discovering Family History)

Research your own family history. Find out if your family had any relatives living in Russia

or on New York's Lower East Side in the early 1900s. Ask family members to write down

what they know about the people and events during this time period. How were your rela-

tives involved directly or indirectly in Jewish communities? Make copies of old drawings or

drawings of keepsakes from this time period.

Documenting History

(Exploring Community History)

Find out how your city or town was affected by Jewish emigration to New York City during the early 1900s. Visit your library, historical society, museum, or local Web site for links to the time period. How did eyewitnesses describe this period in our history? What did newspapers report? When where, why, and how did your community react? Who was involved? What was the result?

Preserving Memories

(Crafting)

Make a scrapbook about Jewish family life in the early 1900s. Imagine what life would be like for your family or for Dimitri's family. Fill the pages with special events, family stories, interviews with relatives, letters, and drawings of family treasures. Add copies of newspaper clippings, photos, postcards, and historical records such as birth certificates and immigration papers. Decorate the pages and the cover with family heirlooms, drawings of Dimitri's violin and gold coins, Hebrew letters and dreidels, or a map showing the journey Dimitri's family or your relatives took by ship from Russia to New York City.

TO FIND OUT MORE

At the Library

Burckhardt, Ann L. *The People of Russia and Their Food.*
Mankato, Minn.: Bridgestone Books, 1996.

Fitterer, C. Ann. *Russian Americans.*
Chanhassen, Minn.: The Child's World, 2003.

Greene, Meg. *The Russian Americans.* Minneapolis: Lucent, 2002.

Hoobler, Dorothy and Thomas. *The Jewish American Family Album.*
New York: Oxford University Press Children's Books, 1998.

Maestro, Betsy. *Coming to America: The Story of Immigration.*
New York: Scholastic, 1996.

On the Internet

Lower East Side
http://www.lowereastsideny.com
For a brief history of the area and a description of current events,
along with a link to historical sites

The Lower East Side Restoration Project
http://www.russiansamovars.com/immigrants.htm
For photos and stories of Russian Jewish families who settled in New York City

The Lower East Side Tenement Museum: Virtual Tour
http://www.tenement.org/Virtual_Tour/index_virtual.html
For a virtual tour of this Orchard Street museum

On the Road

The Eldridge Street Synagogue
12 Eldridge Street
New York, NY 10002
212/219-0903
To visit this Jewish historic landmark erected in 1886

The Jewish Museum
1109 Fifth Avenue
New York, NY 10128
212/423-3200
To learn more about Jewish culture and history

The Lower East Side Tenement Museum
90 Orchard Street
New York, NY 10002
212/431-0233
To learn about the history of New York's Lower East Side

A B O U T   T H E   A U T H O R

Pamela Dell has worked as a writer in many different fields, but what she likes best is inventing characters and telling their stories. She has published fiction for both adults and kids, and in the last half of the 1990s helped found Purple Moon, an acclaimed interactive multimedia company that created CD-ROM games for girls. As writer and lead designer on Purple Moon's award-winning "Rockett" game series, Pamela created the character Rockett Movado and twenty-nine others, and wrote the scripts for each of the series' four episodic games. Purple Moon's Web site, which was based on these characters and their fictional world of Whistling Pines, went on to become one of the largest and most active online communities ever to exist on the Net. Pamela lives in Santa Monica, California, where her favorite fun is still writing fiction and creating cool interactive experiences.